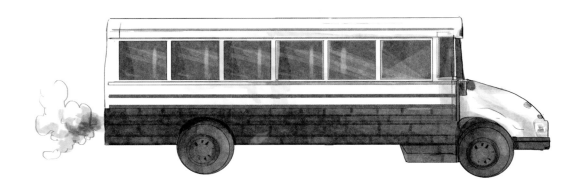

*Skoolie : A school bus that has been purchased and renovated into a mobile tiny home.

My Parents Built a Skoolie

written by Olivia Schlottach

Edited by Rachel Todd

illustrated by Audeva Joseph

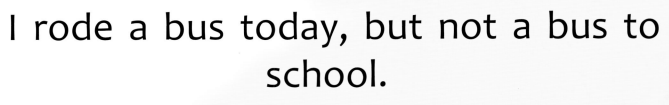

I rode a bus today, but not a bus to school.
I rode a bus that we'll turn into our tiny home, how cool?

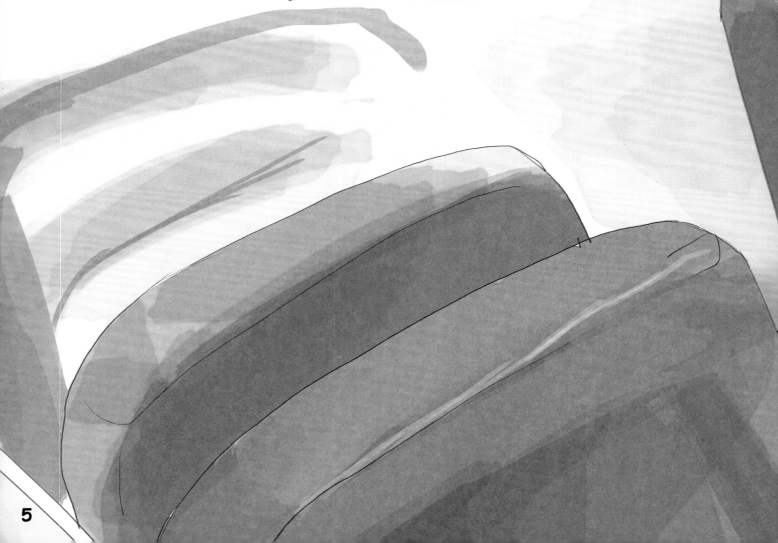

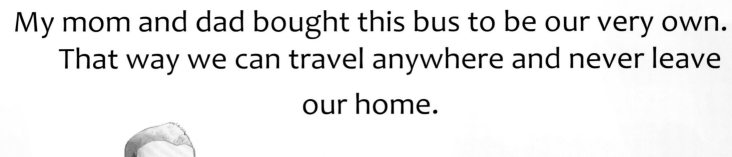

My mom and dad bought this bus to be our very own. That way we can travel anywhere and never leave our home.

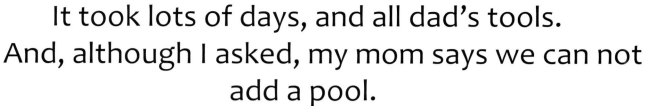

It took lots of days, and all dad's tools.
And, although I asked, my mom says we can not
add a pool.

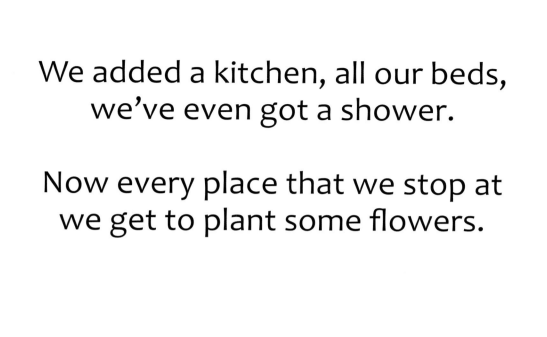

We added a kitchen, all our beds,
we've even got a shower.

Now every place that we stop at
we get to plant some flowers.

We left our home, and our school, and most importantly our friends.
But mom says not to worry, this new adventure never ends.

We can drive our bus anywhere and everywhere we please.
And any time we're hungry we can make our meals with ease.

My baby brother, Keegan,
loved the sand we played in at the beach.
My dad says that he's learning,
the world has got so much to teach.

I swam without my life vest for the first time at Table Rock.
Then I wrote my grandma about the fish we caught off the dock.

I learned to ride my bicycle up in the Smoky Mountains.
We are always on the lookout for my favorite bird the Falcon.

My mom set up an obstacle course
when we went to the Grand Canyon.
I love our Cooper and Mommy time,
she makes the best companion.

16

Traveling on our school bus is the opposite of boring.
How could you get bored when you spend your time exploring?

We drove to California to see the Red Wood Trees. I didn't think I would be impressed but you should see the size of these!

We visit lots of State Parks, up next is Niagara Falls.
My dad says that the plan is for us to see them all.

I lost my first tooth last week, which turns out wasn't so scary.
And even though we are on the road I got a visit from the Fairy.

We broke down on the road today, which mom said can't be good.
But dad put in some work and got our bus running like it should.

Tiny homes may bring less rooms, but to us brings so much more.
It brought us closer to each other and gave us memories that we adore.

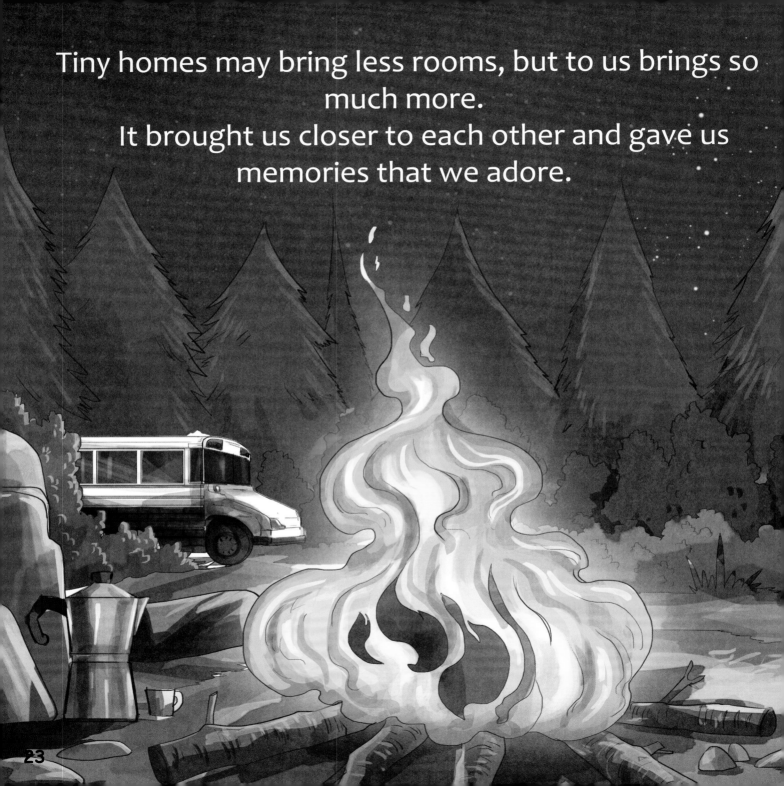

Living on a school bus is not what I expected, truly. But, boy am I so glad that my parents built our Skoolie.